"Promise me you'll always remember:
You're braver than you believe, and stronger than
you seem, and smarter than you think."
– Christopher Robin to Winnie the Pooh

Dear Reader,

My daughter, Gracie, was diagnosed with Leukemia when she was 9 years old. This book is written in her voice, and it'll give you an honest, hopeful and even funny look at what it's really like to kick cancer.

If you or someone you love is battling cancer, we know there is a lot to learn. We hope this book equips and encourages you.

You may feel like you are lost in the dark. But, look up! Hopefully you will see bright, shining stars in the kindness of friends and family that will guide you through this journey.

As you travel, please know you are not alone. We are with you in spirit. Yes, cancer is tough. But together, we are TOUGHER!

Warmest regards and best wishes,
Elizabeth A. Billups

P.S. Check out the glossary and capture your own story and keepsakes in the back of the book. Also, look for tips from our sweet dog, Roo, and keep an eye out for Turtle, who reminds us of the power of courage and determination!

To Gracie, who is bravely enduring more than a child should have to endure – and to her sisters, Josie and Sophie, and her Dad, Val, who are bravely battling alongside her.

To a caring God, our medical team, family, friends and kind strangers who light our way through the darkness.

To the multitude of tenacious researchers and practitioners who are helping us cure cancer.

And to all children and adults who have ever fought or ever will fight cancer … You are brave. You are warriors.

YOU are TOUGHER than cancer!

Elizabeth A. Billups is the author and illustrator, and
Gabriela Schechter is the designer.

The Puddle Jumper's Guide to Kicking Cancer

By Elizabeth A. Billups

Hi there! My name is Gracie. Thanks for reading my story. I hope it helps you.

I am pretty much just a normal kid. I am a soccer player, artist and puddle jumper.

I also have cancer.

Having cancer just means something is growing inside my body that shouldn't be there.

Cancer can grow in anyone ... even very young babies and very old Grandmas and Grandpas.

It can start growing pretty much anywhere in our bodies.

The cancer in my body is growing in my blood. The fancy name for my kind of cancer is "Leukemia."

I have a friend whose cancer is growing in his brain and another friend whose cancer is growing inside her bones.

No matter where the cancer is growing, we've gotta KICK IT OUT!

It was scary to find out I have cancer, but I felt much better when I met my awesome team of doctors and nurses.

They've gone to school for FOREVER to learn the best way to get the cancer OUT of my body, so I will be healthy again.

My doctors and nurses are kinda like my very own cancer-fighting super heroes!

Some people get their cancer removed by a doctor in surgery, and others get special x-rays called "radiation" that wipe out their cancer.

And almost all people fight their cancer with special medicine called "chemotherapy" or "chemo" for short.

I get my chemo in lots of different ways. Sometimes, I have to either swallow pills or drink medicine. It tastes really gross, but I know it's kicking out the cancer so I do it anyway.

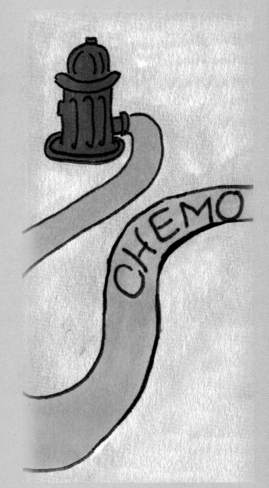

Other times, I have to get shots, and they hurt. But I know the chemo is hurting the cancer more!

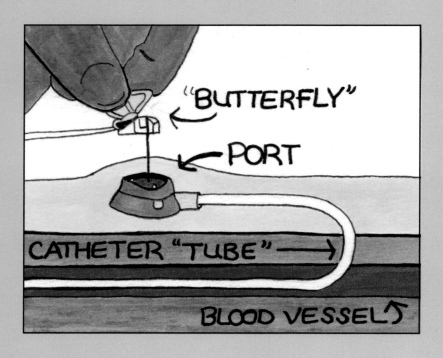

To make it easier to get some of my chemo, my doctor put a special gadget under my skin called a "port."

My nurses are able to put chemo straight into my blood through this port. It's kinda like filling up a jug of water with a hose. The port is just under my skin, below the front of my shoulder.

Now that the skin over the port has healed, I don't even notice it's there. But I'll keep it under my skin until all the cancer is gone. You can't see it, so it's my secret weapon to kick cancer!

Chemo does a great job kicking my cancer out of my body, but the bad news is that chemo also sometimes makes my head hurt or makes me feel sick to my stomach. My doctor gives me medicine that usually helps, but sometimes I still throw up. YUCK!

Some days, it makes me really tired, so I need to rest on the couch and read or watch TV. It's also sometimes hard for me to poop, and I need medicine to "get things moving" as Mom says. So my nurse is always asking me when I last pooped ... which is embarrassing, but also kinda funny!

Other days, I feel totally normal. I get to ride my scooter, go sledding or jump in muddy puddles! Last time I played in the rain, Mom said it reminded her of how I deal with having cancer.

She said, "Some people let rain spoil their whole day. But instead of thinking about what you can't do because of the rain, you find a way to still have fun!"

I love the days when I feel great because I kinda forget that I have cancer for a while and get to just be a normal kid.

I am even happy on these days to get to go back to school. Well ... at least to see my friends and play at recess!

Probably the hardest part of chemo is that it made my hair fall out. Don't worry! It'll grow back, but it was still awful to lose it. I feel different from other kids.

Sometimes I wear hats or a wig.

The wig looks really good, but it's pretty scratchy and hot.

I'll sure be happy when my hair grows back!

Like I said, the chemo does a SUPER job at kicking out my cancer, but it also kicks out some of the parts in my body that help me fight germs. So, it's really easy for me to get sick while I am taking chemo.

Because of this, we all wash our hands ALL the time, and I take more baths or showers.

If I am somewhere really germy while my germ-fighting cells are low, I wear gloves or a mask over my mouth.

Dad says we also need to clean our fruits and veggies in water and vinegar, and I am not allowed to eat left-over food. But that is totally fine by me!

If I get a fever, I need to go to the hospital right away so my doctors can give me medicine to stop my fever. Once I am better, I get to go home again, but sometimes I stay in the hospital overnight for a while. Mom and Dad say it's a good chance to do things I normally don't have enough time to do ... like play cards or learn chess!

Plus, people visit me and usually bring me gifts! I've gotten so many stuffed animals that I have to share them with my sisters.

But it's okay. I know cancer is hard on them, too. Sometimes they have to miss fun activities because I am too sick to go, and my sisters miss Mom and Dad when they stay with me at the hospital.

Even if they don't know how to say it, I know they are sad that I'm sick and want me to get better fast.

So it's only fair that they get to share some of the gifts ... as long as I get to pick the ones I want first!

Kicking cancer is kinda like riding a roller coaster. There are highs and lows.

Sometimes I wonder if it's my fault that I have cancer, but I know it's not anyone's fault. There are just times when bad things happen for no reason at all.

Of course, it's hard on Mom and Dad, too. I've even seen them cry because they are sad that I have to go through all of this.

And there are times I feel sad, too ... and times I feel MAD, and I want to SCREAM!

One time Mom and I both felt like screaming, so you know what? We did! We just started screaming and shouting ... and then actually ended up laughing!

Since kicking cancer is hard work for our whole family, Mom and Dad make sure we still do a lot of fun things together.

It's great to know I don't need to kick cancer all on my own. My family and friends are with me every step of the way.

We may not like that I have cancer, but LOVE is what's helping me kick it!

Thanks for reading my story. If you or someone you love has cancer, I hope my story helps you. I know it might seem like a sad story, but I like to think of it as an adventure story.

There are times when it's hard and times when I get tired of taking my medicine, getting shots or feeling sick.

But it's like the story about the little train who needed to climb the TALL mountain to bring good food and toys to the kids on the other side.

I am kinda like that little train. I have to do something I've never done before. It's a little scary, and I have to be brave and do it anyway.

But I am not alone. I have a huge team of doctors, nurses, pastors, family, friends and even people I haven't ever met helping me get over this mountain and kick cancer.

Yes, cancer is tough ... but
TOGETHER WE ARE TOUGHER!

Glossary of Terms

Absolute Neutrophil Count (ANC) is a measure of the number of neutrophils in the blood. Neutrophils are a type of white blood cell that fights against infection.

Bone Marrow is the spongy center inside of bones where blood cells are made. They begin as stem cells. Stem cells become red blood cells, white blood cells and platelets in the marrow. Then the red blood cells, white blood cells and platelets enter the blood.

Biopsy is the removal of a sample of tissue from the body for further examination. A biopsy gives doctors a closer look at what's going on inside to help make a diagnosis and choose the right treatment.

Bone Marrow Transplant (BMT) is a procedure that involves replacing unhealthy bone marrow with healthy bone marrow cells from a donor.

CAT scan (also a CT scan) is a type of x-ray in which a machine rotates around the patient and creates a picture of the inside of the body from different angles. Regular x-rays show bones and other areas of the body, but CAT scans show much more detail.

Cerebrospinal fluid (CSF) is a clear, colorless liquid that delivers nutrients to and "cushions" the brain and spinal cord (the central nervous system). It's important to put chemo into the CSF because Leukemia cells like to hide out in the CSF.

Chemotherapy (chemo) is a collection of medicine given to people with cancer to stop or slow the growth of cancer cells, which grow and divide quickly. It can also harm healthy cells that divide quickly, such as those that line your mouth and intestines or cause your hair to grow.

Hemoglobin is the protein inside red blood cells that carries oxygen.

Intravenous (IV) means "within a vein." Most often it refers to giving medicines or fluids through a needle or tube inserted into a vein. This allows the medicine or fluid to enter your bloodstream right away. For example, your health care provider may prescribe medicines to be given through a vein, or an intravenous (IV) line.

Magnetic Resonance Imaging (MRI) is a safe and painless test that uses a magnetic field and radio waves to produce detailed pictures of the body's organs and structures.

Neutropenia occurs when a person has a low level of neutrophils, a type of white blood cell. This is measured by the Absolute Neutrophil Count (ANC). All white blood cells help the body fight infection. Neutrophils fight infection by destroying harmful bacteria and fungi or yeast that invade the body. Neutrophils are made in the bone marrow. People who have neutropenia have a higher risk of developing serious infections. This is because they do not have enough neutrophils to destroy organisms that cause infection.

Plasma is the liquid part of the blood. It is mostly water. It also has some vitamins, minerals, proteins, hormones and other natural chemicals in it.

Platelets are the part of the blood that forms plugs that help stop bleeding at the site of an injury.

Port is a small device that is used with a central line. The port is placed under the skin of the chest. After the site heals, no dressings and no special home care are needed. The doctor or nurse can give medicines or nutrition or take blood samples. He or she puts a needle through the skin into the port. A numbing cream can be put on the skin before the port is used.

Red Blood Cells (RBC) carry oxygen around the body. When the number of red blood cells is below normal, the condition is called anemia. Anemia may make you feel tired or short of breath. It may make the skin look pale.

Radiation therapy (also called radiotherapy, irradiation, or x-ray therapy) is one of the most common forms of cancer treatment. In radiation therapy, high-energy radiation from x-rays, gamma rays, or other sources is used to kill cancer cells and shrink tumors. Radiation therapy prevents cells from growing or reproducing by destroying them.

Remission occurs when evidence of cancer disappears.

Spinal tap (lumbar puncture) is a medical procedure in which a needle is inserted into the spinal canal, to collect spinal fluid samples or distribute medicine into the spinal fluid.

Ultrasound (also called sonography) is another way doctors can take a look inside the body. Instead of x-rays, sound waves are bounced off the kidneys, the heart, or other areas of the body.

White Blood Cells (WBC) fight infection in the body. There are two major types of white blood cells: neutrophils and lymphocytes.

Here are some pages for you to tell YOUR story!

Circle the face that best describes how you felt when you found out you or someone you care about has cancer.

Draw a picture or write about your feelings.

"Star Moments"

When we have fun moments during sad times, these moments are kinda like stars shining in a dark night. It could be a special gift you got, or it could be anything that made you feel loved during a hard time, such as a hug, a fun activity with a friend, or a cool surprise. Draw or describe your special "star moments."

Tough Times

Ever heard of the expression "better out than in"? It means that it's better to tell someone when you feel sad, mad, scared or confused instead of keeping these yucky feelings trapped inside your head. Trust me! You'll feel better after you talk about how you feel with someone you love.

Draw or describe things that make you feel
sad, mad, scared or confused.

When you are a Grandma or Grandpa, what do you think you'll remember about this time in your life?

Draw a picture or describe your thoughts here.

Memory Scrapbook

Use the next few pages to tape or glue anything you want to keep that will remind you of this time in your life. You'll probably want to look at these reminders when you are a grown up! You could save a hospital bracelet, pictures, special cards, or a list of your favorite visitors, gifts, or activities.

79084879R00022

Made in the USA
Lexington, KY
17 January 2018